WHERE ARE THEY?

FIND FREDDIE & LISA IN THE HAUNTED HOUSE

BY
ANTHONY TALLARICO

SMITHMARK

Copyright © 1991 Kidsbooks Inc. and Anthony Tallarico
7004 N. California Ave.
Chicago, IL 60645

This edition published in 1991 by SMITHMARK Publishers Inc.,
112 Madison Avenue, New York, NY 10016

ISBN: 0-8317-4361-1

SMITHMARK books are available for bulk purchase for sales promotion and premium use.
For details write or telephone the Manager of Special Sales, SMITHMARK Publishers Inc.,
112 Madison Avenue, New York, NY 10016. (212) 532-6600.
Manufactured in the United States of America

Freddie and Lisa have discovered a house that's unlike any other...a haunted house!

FIND FREDDIE & LISA AT THE HAUNTED HOUSE AND...

- ☐ Apples (2)
- ☐ Apron
- ☐ Baseball cap
- ☐ Bats (2)
- ☐ Bones (3)
- ☐ Box
- ☐ Burned-out candle
- ☐ Clothespin
- ☐ Coffeepot
- ☐ Crown
- ☐ Dog
- ☐ Dracula
- ☐ Duck
- ☐ Eyeglasses
- ☐ Faucet
- ☐ Fish tank
- ☐ Fishing pole
- ☐ Ghosts (3)
- ☐ Hammer
- ☐ Heart
- ☐ Kite
- ☐ Light bulb
- ☐ Lips
- ☐ Mouse
- ☐ Mummy
- ☐ Owl
- ☐ Paint bucket
- ☐ Paper bag
- ☐ Peanut
- ☐ Pencils (2)
- ☐ Piggy bank
- ☐ Question mark
- ☐ Saw
- ☐ Scarves (2)
- ☐ Sock
- ☐ Straw
- ☐ Submarine
- ☐ Tire
- ☐ Truck
- ☐ Umbrella

Should they go in?
Should they not go in?
What do you think
they should do?

FIND FREDDIE &
LISA BEFORE
THEY DECIDE
AND...

☐ Birds (2)
☐ Black paint
☐ Blimps (2)
☐ Bowling ball
☐ Box
☐ Broom
☐ Burned-out bulb
☐ Cactus
☐ Camel
☐ Candle
☐ Chef's hat
☐ Feather
☐ Flower
☐ Football
☐ Giant straw
☐ Giraffe
☐ Jester
☐ King
☐ Laundry
☐ License plate
☐ Longest hair
☐ Lost boot
☐ Lost mask
☐ Mustache
☐ Napoleon
☐ Painted egg
☐ Rabbit
☐ Rain cloud
☐ Red wagon
☐ Sailboat
☐ Short pants
☐ Skull
☐ Sled
☐ Slide
☐ Star
☐ Top hats (2)
☐ Trash can
☐ Umbrella
☐ Who can't go?

Ready...Set...Go!!
Everyone runs toward
the door of the haunted
house...but only
two enter!

FIND FREDDIE & LISA AS THEY MEET THE MONSTERS AND...

☐ Apple
☐ Arrow
☐ Bag
☐ Balloon
☐ Banana peel
☐ Baseball cap
☐ Bodiless head
☐ Bone
☐ Boot
☐ Bows (3)
☐ Broken heart
☐ Broom
☐ Cake
☐ Can
☐ Candles (5)
☐ Clothesline
☐ Crystal ball
☐ Earrings
☐ Eyeglasses
☐ Fish
☐ Flower
☐ Four-eyed monster
☐ Genie
☐ Ghosts (2)
☐ Ice-cream cone
☐ Lightning
☐ Necktie
☐ Number 13
☐ Owl
☐ Piano
☐ Roller skates
☐ Santa Claus
☐ Six-fingered hand
☐ Skulls (5)
☐ Snake
☐ Spoon
☐ Tombstone
☐ Watering can
☐ Worms (2)

Ms. Witch makes monstrous snacks. Her specialty is the "Everything Goes" sandwich!

FIND FREDDIE & LISA AT SNACK TIME AND...

- ☐ Accordion
- ☐ Apple
- ☐ Baseball
- ☐ Bell
- ☐ Blackbird
- ☐ Bone
- ☐ Brush
- ☐ Candle
- ☐ Checkerboard
- ☐ Drill
- ☐ Earring
- ☐ Faucet
- ☐ Fish (2)
- ☐ Flower
- ☐ Fork
- ☐ Frying pan
- ☐ Grapes
- ☐ Green cup
- ☐ Heart
- ☐ Helmet
- ☐ Ice-cream cone
- ☐ Ladle
- ☐ Mustaches (2)
- ☐ Neckties (2)
- ☐ Oil can
- ☐ Orange
- ☐ Palm tree
- ☐ Pear
- ☐ Polka-dotted handkerchief
- ☐ Rolling pin
- ☐ Saw
- ☐ Scissors
- ☐ Sock
- ☐ Stool
- ☐ Straw
- ☐ Toaster
- ☐ TV set
- ☐ Watermelon
- ☐ Wooden spoon

Freddie & Lisa begin to explore the haunted house. A wrong turn and...down, down, down they tumble.

FIND FREDDIE & LISA IN THE DUNGEON AND...

- ☐ Airplane
- ☐ Balloon
- ☐ Banana peel
- ☐ Bomb
- ☐ Book
- ☐ Bowling ball
- ☐ Broken egg
- ☐ Broom
- ☐ Candy cane
- ☐ Corn
- ☐ Cupcake
- ☐ Doctor
- ☐ Drum
- ☐ Fire hydrant
- ☐ Flowerpot
- ☐ Flying bat
- ☐ Football
- ☐ Hammer
- ☐ Hot dog
- ☐ Ice-cream cone
- ☐ Ice-cream pop
- ☐ Mummies (3)
- ☐ Piggy bank
- ☐ Rabbit
- ☐ Racer
- ☐ Roller skates
- ☐ Scarecrow
- ☐ School bag
- ☐ Shark
- ☐ Showerhead
- ☐ Skateboard
- ☐ Skulls (2)
- ☐ Skunk
- ☐ Sock
- ☐ Star
- ☐ Swing
- ☐ Top hat
- ☐ Trash can
- ☐ Trumpet
- ☐ Umbrellas (2)
- ☐ Wagon

Next to the dungeon are the wildest lanes in town. It's a great place to do anything—but bowl!

FIND FREDDIE & LISA AT THE GHOSTLY BOWLING ALLEY AND...

Dr. Frankenstein has lots of patients who need lots of patience.

FIND FREDDIE & LISA IN DR. FRANKENSTEIN'S LABORATORY AND...

☐ Black cat
☐ Book
☐ Bow tie
☐ Bride
☐ Bunny fiend
☐ Candle
☐ Cheese
☐ Dog
☐ Dracula
☐ Duck
☐ Feather
☐ Greeting card
☐ Hot hat
☐ Ice-cream pop
☐ Invisible person
☐ Neckerchief
☐ Paintbrush
☐ Paint bucket
☐ Pickax
☐ Roller skates
☐ Sailor fiend
☐ Saw
☐ Screwdriver
☐ Shovel
☐ Skull
☐ Suspenders
☐ Thing-in-a-sack
☐ Three-eyed creature
☐ Three-legged thing
☐ Toothbrush
☐ Tulip
☐ TV set
☐ Two-headed thing
☐ Watch
☐ Who has a sore throat?
☐ Who has a toothache?
☐ Who needs a haircut?
☐ Who snores?
☐ Who's been shrunk?
☐ Who's on a diet?
☐ Wooden block

"Dinner is served!"
Fortunately, the
skeletons don't eat much.

FIND FREDDIE &
LISA AT THE
DINNER PARTY
AND...

- ☐ Arrow
- ☐ Ax
- ☐ Baseball bat
- ☐ Bird
- ☐ Birdcage
- ☐ Bodiless head
- ☐ Bucket
- ☐ Candles (3)
- ☐ Cat in a hat
- ☐ Cat wearing a hat
- ☐ Deer
- ☐ Dieter
- ☐ Dog
- ☐ Duck
- ☐ Elephant
- ☐ Feathers (2)
- ☐ Fish bones
- ☐ Fork
- ☐ Frankfurter
- ☐ Giraffe
- ☐ Grapes
- ☐ Headless body
- ☐ Heart
- ☐ High-heel shoes
- ☐ Horse
- ☐ Invisible person
- ☐ Mouse
- ☐ Mummies (2)
- ☐ Neckties (2)
- ☐ One-eyed monster
- ☐ Painted egg
- ☐ Pencil
- ☐ Robot
- ☐ Scarves (2)
- ☐ Target
- ☐ Tennis racket
- ☐ Thermometer
- ☐ Three-legged chair
- ☐ Tieless waiter
- ☐ Umbrella
- ☐ Yo-yo

After dinner, Freddie and Lisa explore a junk-filled room upstairs. There they find someone who <u>really</u> knows how to save!

FIND FREDDIE & LISA IN DRACULA'S ATTIC AND...

- ☐ Book
- ☐ Boomerang
- ☐ Broom
- ☐ Calendar
- ☐ Candy cane
- ☐ Chef's hat
- ☐ Clocks (2)
- ☐ Cracked mirror
- ☐ Fire hydrant
- ☐ Garden hose
- ☐ Golf club
- ☐ Ice-cream cone
- ☐ Key
- ☐ Moon
- ☐ Mouse
- ☐ Necklace
- ☐ Necktie
- ☐ Oar
- ☐ Old-fashioned radio
- ☐ Paint bucket
- ☐ Paper airplane
- ☐ Pencil
- ☐ Pyramid
- ☐ Santa's hat
- ☐ Saw
- ☐ Skateboard
- ☐ Skulls (4)
- ☐ Slice of pizza
- ☐ Spray can
- ☐ Stocking
- ☐ Straw
- ☐ String of pearls
- ☐ Stuffed panda
- ☐ Target
- ☐ Telephone booth
- ☐ Top hat
- ☐ Train engine
- ☐ Viking helmet
- ☐ Wagon wheel
- ☐ Wig
- ☐ Yarn

The monsters walk very carefully when they visit <u>this</u> room!

FIND FREDDIE & LISA IN THE COBWEB ROOM AND...

- ☐ Baby carriage
- ☐ Bats (2)
- ☐ Binoculars
- ☐ Boot
- ☐ Bow tie
- ☐ Boxing glove
- ☐ Broom
- ☐ Cup
- ☐ Dog
- ☐ Duck
- ☐ Earring
- ☐ Electric plug
- ☐ Fish
- ☐ Flower
- ☐ Football helmet
- ☐ Fork
- ☐ Ghosts (2)
- ☐ Hammer
- ☐ Heart
- ☐ Key
- ☐ Kite
- ☐ Lock
- ☐ Moon face
- ☐ Mummy
- ☐ Number 13
- ☐ Old-fashioned radio
- ☐ Paintbrush
- ☐ Pencil
- ☐ Ring
- ☐ Robot
- ☐ Screwdriver
- ☐ Ship
- ☐ Six-fingered creature
- ☐ Skull
- ☐ Spider
- ☐ Top hat
- ☐ Train engine
- ☐ Turtles (2)
- ☐ Umbrella
- ☐ Wagon

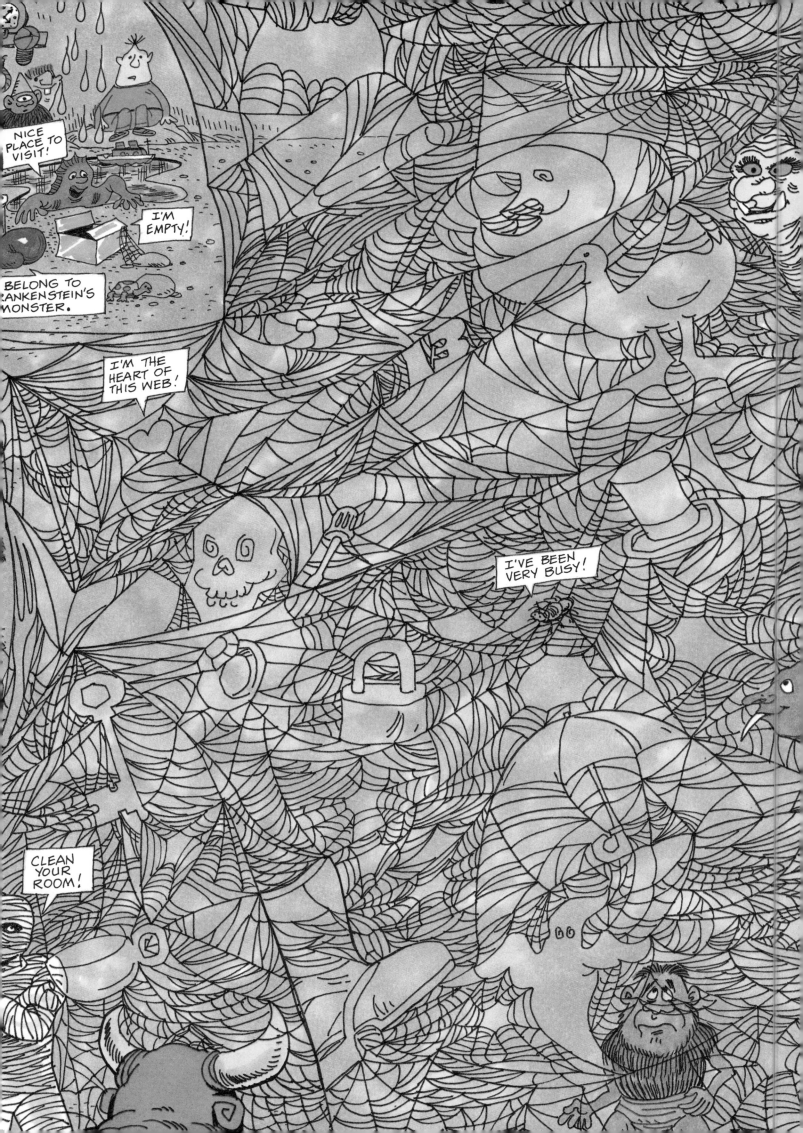

Freddie & Lisa find a great place to play. Anyone can have fun here!

FIND FREDDIE & LISA IN THE MONSTERS' PLAYROOM AND...

- ☐ Artist
- ☐ Balloon
- ☐ Banana peel
- ☐ Barbell
- ☐ Beanie
- ☐ Birds (2)
- ☐ Blackboard
- ☐ Crayons (5)
- ☐ Donkey
- ☐ Fish
- ☐ Football
- ☐ Haunted house
- ☐ Hole in the head
- ☐ Hood
- ☐ Ice skate
- ☐ Jack-o'-lanterns (4)
- ☐ Jacks (4)
- ☐ Joke book
- ☐ Juggler
- ☐ Loose change
- ☐ Mask
- ☐ Monster-in-the-box
- ☐ Monster puppet
- ☐ Mummy doll
- ☐ Musician
- ☐ Nail
- ☐ Pail
- ☐ "Pin-the-tail-on-the-donkey"
- ☐ Pogo stick
- ☐ Rubber ducky
- ☐ Sailboat
- ☐ Snake
- ☐ Telephone
- ☐ Tepee
- ☐ Three-legged thing
- ☐ Tricycle
- ☐ Truck
- ☐ Turtle
- ☐ TV set
- ☐ Who attends "Horror U"?
- ☐ Wind-up monster

Mummy is in her favorite place, making something from an old family recipe.

FIND FREDDIE & LISA IN MUMMY'S KITCHEN AND...

It's time for Freddie & Lisa to go. The friendly monsters hope their new friends will return soon.

FIND FREDDIE & LISA LEAVING THE HAUNTED HOUSE AND...

- ☐ Apple
- ☐ Arrow
- ☐ Balloon
- ☐ Birds (2)
- ☐ Box
- ☐ Broken heart
- ☐ Brooms (2)
- ☐ Candles (2)
- ☐ Clock
- ☐ Crown
- ☐ Did they have fun?
- ☐ Dog
- ☐ Duck
- ☐ Envelope
- ☐ Feather
- ☐ Firecracker
- ☐ Flower
- ☐ Ice skates
- ☐ Jack-o'-lanterns (4)
- ☐ Key
- ☐ Ladder
- ☐ Lamp
- ☐ Moon face
- ☐ Mouse
- ☐ Painted egg
- ☐ Periscope
- ☐ Rabbit
- ☐ Roller skates
- ☐ Scarves (3)
- ☐ Seven-fingered creature
- ☐ Shovel
- ☐ Skull
- ☐ Straw
- ☐ Tick-Tack-Toe
- ☐ Top hat
- ☐ Tree
- ☐ TV camera
- ☐ Umbrella
- ☐ When will they return?
- ☐ Which exit did they use?
- ☐ Who will miss them the most?
- ☐ Who doesn't use toothpaste?

Freddie and Lisa are
here with a few of their
playmates.

Donald   Hector
Frankie   Susie
Laura   Bunny Honey
Sam   Santa
Santa's helpers — Fee, Fi, Fo and Fun